morbid lovers

I0445354

love

Samantha

August

Morbid Lovers

by Samantha August

ISBN-13: 978-0692230008 (Morbid Lovers)

Dedication

To my Loves. To my heart song.

To our free spirited children.

To my whole family.

~XO

Ours was just another inter departmental romance: A 911 dispatcher and a 5-O. **POPO**. A Cop. I never thought for one moment that I would be an officer's wife.

We met, we fell in deep. Deep and madly in love. And life was beautiful.

Until I heard him die.

My name is Samantha August, and this is my story.

"Everything that happens before death is what counts"

- Ray Bradbury

Forward

I HAD loved this bed. I didn't ever want to get out of it. I reached over for JT and he wasn't there.

PLEASE DON'T DIE. PLEASE please don't leave me. Please don't DIE.

I rolled over, and quickly fell back to sleep. I was having a nightmare. No biggie.

I hit the snooze 4 times. It was time to wake up or I would be late. People depend on you Sam, you have to wake up. They need you.

WAKE UP.

If you go to work, he will die on you. It's the way the game goes. The "Rat Race". It's how it goes.

Help people, save people. One day at a time. One reckless soul at a time. Love people, HATE PEOPLE.

HE DIED that night in the patrol car.

1

Before Death

There was a leftover scent from JT, my man, my lover. So clean, so fresh. It intoxicated me. He always kissed me goodbye before he ran out the door. He had to be to work one hour before me.

I was so alone in bed without him. I just wanted to be near him. Hear his heart beat again.

I had to prep for a crazy night, so why not start out in a total ZEN way?

Nope- not how I work. It's PANIC MODE or nothing!

When I am stressed, I dump deeper in stress. It's how I roll. SINK OR SWIM.

It is very rare in the Emergency Services field to find someone who IS NOT sleep deprived.

"Oh Sleep, Oh sleep

Nature's Soft Nurse!"

—Shakespeare

Night time is when evil lurks.

Morbidity, death, hate, fear, EXTREME EVIL.

I thought to myself; something I have stated more times in my life than anything else.

"911. What's the address of you emergency?"

There was never a silent moment, and at times it was ravenous. It's the perfect career for a crazy, wild spirited, helper junkie such as I. You mustn't tame the wicked.

This thought instantaneously over-whelmed me.

I have to find my pills. Where are my pills? Where the FUCK are my pills?

I finally located my pill bottle, which had fallen in between my bed, and the nightstand. Today was definitely an-other pill popping day. There really hadn't been an unmedicated moment in my career.

Many thoughts were always invading my mind. This led to a wild ride, yet easier way to deal with the fucked up world. Please prep to COMBAT the COMBATive.

PREP SAM, prep.

There was never a moment that the thought of doing something else with my life didn't cross my mind.

The drugs I was about to induce helped me with my crazy feelings. I had felt that I was God's hands and feet. But when something terrible happens over and over, and over again you tend to label yourself. I labeled myself as tired, failure, loser, co-dependent freak. Lack of sleep contributed to my over exhausted mental state.

I was so tired. Sooo lost in life. I wanted to stay home and be a homemaker. I wanted to have all the money in the world so he didn't have to do this job anymore. He has already saved me, why does he need to save anyone else? HE and I were not fighting the evils of this world ANYMORE!

It wasn't unusual for me to get 4-6 hours of sleep. When I really needed 12!

Please kick in drugs, I have to keep the street guys safe! I have to send help to those in need. Fuck, I seriously hate people.

Why? Why am I doing this to myself. A recent diagnosis of it's time to retire, and go do something for yourself, was replaying over and over in my mind as I forced myself to look in the mirror.

I grabbed my water bottle, swallowed my prescribed narcs and took a thankful deep breath. I looked at the mirror and reminded myself of something I had wrote above me in black eyeliner. "Thank you GOD, Universe, Keeper of my soul. I am your hands and feet, CARRY THE PAIN so I don't have to."

These drugs kept me sane, and energized. After all, I was a SILENT HERO. I was "America's Lifeline to Safety".

I darted around my tiny dark room grabbing the cleanest professional clothes I had. It didn't usually matter what I wore on graves because we didn't run into brass.

I had to search for my favorite bra, yet again. It was usually misplaced after beer breakfast or choir practice (a graveyard shift after party). JT and I usually indulged in a rather large breakfast burrito, and some delicious whiskey. I acted tough, I actually hated whiskey. I sure loved the way it felt. It was a sudden release for me to feel the warm, burning sensation, slipping down my throat. Two to three sips later the intense emotions that lingered from the shift before usually subsided.

JT had usually forced me to eat. I never had an appetite on any shift. He was usually irritated that I didn't care for my body the way I should. After all, he went to nursing school, only later to become part of "Big Brother". These whiskey breakfasts quickly turned in to a multiple orgasmic experience.

Orgasms at the same time were a regular practice of ours. It was something I had never experienced with anyone else. He knew how to please me.

Was this his age? His life experience? Or was this a complete spiritual experience?

Who knows? All I know was I liked it. I LOVED it. I just couldn't believe it, he was mine.

I gave my dark out of control, just been fucked hair, a quick brush. I grabbed the closest black hair tie and put it up in a quick sloppy bun.

Mmm, I love this expensive shine serum that I used. It smelled so good! I loved using the leftover serum in my palms and would gently apply it to my elbows, and massaged the rest in my hands. It made my hands so soft.

I hair-sprayed my out of control fly aways. I quickly tidied up my eye make-up, and dabbed on my favorite Dr. Pepper Lip Chap.

Damn, I am a mess. I grabbed my phone to check the time. I was hoping I would have time to spoon up to JT before we had a shit storm to deal with.

Spooning up was just another police term. He would pull his car up to my car, his driver side against mine. Yes, I know… Sounds sexual. But it wasn't. I just wanted to see his face.

You could say that my JT fit the pro-file of most cops. He was 5'10 and weighed 190 pounds. He was lean yet, strong. I loved his legs.

Weird, I know? He had really nice calves. He had sex appeal, yet had a romance about him that I can't seem to get weened from.

My thoughts usually got a hold of me before any shift. I looked at my cell and saw the time.

Shit! 20 minutes till briefing! FUCK! I couldn't be late.

There had never been a moment that had gone by that a crazy thought didn't come into my mind.

One time, I had gone to my OBG-YN. I had left the penthouse suite office on the 9th floor and entered the elevator. I found myself surrounded by many successful doctors.

They all must have held their high paying practices in this building. I prayed silently to myself and asked the Universal God to build an imaginary bullet proof wall. A wall that would protect them from my mental thoughts. Protect them from me. Me from them. I didn't really like people anymore. They hurt others. They did not have any compassion.

I also assumed that had they heard what I was thinking, they would institutionalize me.

I looked at doctor number one and thought that he was a complete freaking creep. He definitely molested his patients. I continued to look at the other well defined men. The way one of them had been looking at the other with a lustful gaze was evident to me that they had a little outside romance going on.

You could tell that he wasn't living the life he wanted. He had a counterfeit nature about him. He wore a very thin gold wedding band and was showing pictures of his kids to one of the other doctors. I had thought to myself that he was gay and needed to leave his wife. He was a weird Christian FREAK.

I didn't understand why people were so caught up in the church and their fraudulent identities, that they couldn't live like they truly wanted to.

I looked at the other guy and had a simple thought of how tasty he would be! He could easily replace my OBG-YN.

It turned out, I had no filter. The thought escaped my mind and turned to weird words.

"I guess if we all crashed, I'd most likely make it since I am surrounded by DOCS!"

Laughter had filled the elevator. Thank goodness.

JT and I had shared this same morbid sense of humor.

ANYWAYS- all this was my subliminal pep talk to get myself to work. I jumped in the car. Turned on music and drove.

on scene

I could finally see the Police Department. I had 5 minutes to spare.

"UGH! I wished Starbucks was open. I NEED NEED COFFEE!!!"

JT made the best coffee for me when he didn't have to work. There were two days that we didn't work together. Which was enjoyable. He had time to relax and do his thing. On my days off, I took care of my kiddos.

We did not have a mutual day off. This stunk. We would see each other in passing. We always made time for each other. Whether it was working out at the gym, or coffee dates at Starbucks before our shifts.

We had to learn to not talk about work when we were together. That was the hardest part of our relationship. Tell me of a couple that doesn't talk about work with each other?

The PD was gorgeous at night. It was right off the highway. It was well lit. You could see it from a mile away. It could easily be a target for a terrorist.

The window's to the 2nd story, where the 911 center was, had bullet holes. Someone in the field across from highway was the culprit. Somehow, never caught. Not that a busy department had time to investigate such things.

The madness in me believes it was a still employed, pissed off, Police Officer.

I assumed that this was an attempt to shoot a mindless, gum chewing, deaf, fat ass, argumentative dispatcher in the head. Thank you tax payers, you contributed to this multi million dollar building and bullet proof glass.

I grabbed my key fob out of my glove box. If command Staff had known I kept it there, I'd most likely get reprimanded.

FINALLY ON SCENE.

It's extremely difficult to find a dispatcher who could make it past three months, let alone 10 years. I asked the universe for a new job daily. A single mother such as I, had no business finding a new job. It wasn't JT's responsibility to take care of all of us on his own. After all, baby daddy didn't give me a dime.

I'm grateful for my incredible children, but fuck, the sperm donor is enough to drive a sane woman such as I, completely mad. Wait, I went mad a long time ago.

I'd practically raised the babies completely zombiefied on my days off. No help from him.

I'd usually have to miss out on a complete day of sleep. I worked a horrid shift! 0200-1000 with Monday's and Tuesday's off.

The majority of the department was staffed by men. It never failed that I'd get my daily- DAMN, check that chick out!

I cringed thinking about the assholes who looked at me and soaked me up. I was frequently reminded during patrol briefings. This irritated JT but he knew he held the key to my soul. He knew his girl wasn't going anywhere.

Depending on the shift, and how long I had know the guys on the streets, I would usually have to convince them that I was an awesome dispatcher, and not just a piece of ass. However, I had my fair share of big brothers at the PD looking out for me.

I scanned the key fob against the black magnetic card reader.

I entered the first door.

I had to repeat the same routine daily. I entered in through the 2nd door. I continued to the door which was directly through the lobby and behind the bullet proof glass sat a familiar face. Just another guy at the police department that wanted a little taste of my ass.

The "other guys" I worked with wouldn't want me anyways, I was taken! Not to mention being protected by my man, and ALL of his friends.

I couldn't blame him for looking, after all, we didn't make our relationship public information.

Fuck you "guy" who thinks you are allowed to look at me. I have lives to save.

You wouldn't want me anyways, I was taken. My man was a secret. My little secret. JT could easily beat the shit out of any one of them.

As usual, I gave a quick wave as I displayed a tortuous fake smile and went on my way.

I had 3 MINUTES to get my stuff from my locker and log in to ALL 5 computers.

pretty girl

I've definitely been described as pretty. I am 5'4 and a half. Yes an added half. I have gorgeous green eyes, I'd say this is my asset. Much like superstars insure their body parts, I'd insure my eyes.

Haha!

My green eyes are quickly complimented by my long, black eye lashes. I have olive colored skin, naturally blushed pink cheeks, and chocolate brown hair. I made sure my hair was regularly dyed. I hated the natural red streaks that would pop out occasionally.

I got these from my alcoholic father. It must have been all the Fire Ball he drank habitually.

We mustn't forget my gorgeous straight white teeth. I humbly speak- with hard-core humor. I'm 100% German. Unlike my blonde haired, blue eyed siblings- I wouldn't have survived The Holocaust. I would have easily been mistaken for a Jew.

I never had allowed anyone to look into my eyes since my kid's dad. I felt that my eyes held the key that led straight to my heart. My heart leads directly into the deepest part of my soul. This area needed serious protection.

I always hired imaginaries best. A team of security officials and surveillance officers protecting it with AR-15 Rifles, and S&W 1911's. A staff of blood thirsty vampires, and an entire Chinese Army. Wait! One more to add; an entire S.W.A.T. team. After all, this was a heavily burdened, broken heart. I had to protect it.

But somehow, he snuck in. He saw the real me. Everything universally clicked. Every single bit of my journey, led me straight to him, and him straight to me.

Oh JT. He was always on my mind.

He'd grab my face and stare into my eyes. I'd shutter with fear. I called upon all of my little Guard Gnomes, and all the other security officials I had mentally hired. I was scared to death. There was no way- NO WAY at all, I would not let him in. If I let him in- he'd HURT me.

He'd look at me with his dark brown eyes. He'd touch me. He'd grab my face and pull it close to him.

FUCK ME, he's got me. He's got me so INFATUATED. TWISTED. He had won the war to my heart.

When I first met JT, I could not stop talking to him. He was hilarious. He was smart, he was genuine. He was the person that a lot of people wanted to be around.

I called JT and asked him what he was up to. Not because I was trying to hit on him, mostly because I wanted his friendship. He didn't seem to WANT me, like every other guy I had got to know.

The problem here, is that I got to know men. But in the emergency industry it is very hard to get to know women. They are tough, and usually were in the same boat as I. It's hard to make it as a female.

I joked once while I had to go on a mandatory fire ride along. Usually ride alongs were considered "RIDE ONS". It never failed that when I would get back, a dispatcher would want to know what guy I fucked or had got to know.

NONE YUH.

While on this ride along, the Engineer on the bus (the big red truck) was a female. I was completely relieved. We had been dispatched to an emergent medical call.

We all jumped in and I was told to put my headphones on so we could all chat with each other. The crew was awesome.

"Hey Sam, why haven't you been out with us on a ride before?"

The noise from the sirens on the engine were still blaring in the background.

"Well, to be completely honest, it's frowned upon when you are a dispatcher. Usually it gets rumored that I had a love affair with the entire department, thank GOD there is a female on this engine. I can go back without any fuck stains. Oh- and it's mandatory by the boss."

Everyone started laughing.

"It's true!"

The engine crew continued to laugh, and joke, they knew how it was. Slutty dispatchers.

"Well, Sam, bad news. I am a lesbian. You aren't safe here with this crew."

Haha! I loved it. I love real people with crude sense of humor. Had I been fucked in an engine before? NO. It's a fantasy for many. Had I been fucked in a patrol car? NO.

I'd prefer to respect the uniform. I'd prefer to not be a Badge Bunny.

So back to my first meet up with JT.

I called him, and asked him where he was. At that time, in 2010, I was abstaining from sex. Working on myself. Or trying to that is.

It was genuine. I wanted JT as my friend. Nothing more.

He answered the phone, and said he was at the Starbucks nearby.

"I'm just dropping off my kids, want me to meet you? I am really close."

"Sure, I am sitting at the coffee bar."

I walked in and saw him with a Venti size cup of coffee. He wasn't dressed up in million dollar clothing. He was a t-shirt and jeans kind of guy. I found this sexy.

Wait Sam, remember? Friendships. Work on you. I wasn't being honest with myself. I was an actress. I just was abstaining from sex, not my multiple relationships. I was actually dating 5 guys when I met JT. I became good at my balancing act.

JT and I hit it off. We talked and talked. I ended up learning from him that I was doing what I was doing because I was running from my guilt.

JT and I had much more in common than I had realized.

I ended up crying on our first "meet". He knew me. We talked about our kid's parents. We talked about our kids. We talked about how we both had loved our exes very much, and the pain we went through when we got divorced. And not to mention the horrific pain we felt when our kids weren't with us. He actually wanted to help me through it.

I showed him my messy trunk. It still held my past baggage. No way was I bringing my broken dreams in to my new house. I drove them around in my car.

I told him about my recent en-counter with the "STALLION".

Big mistake. Don't ever talk to your man about their bosses and having sex with them. Also, don't describe to them the girth that penis' can have when they are hard. Guys in the PD walk around naked in the locked room.

4

heart song

JT and I hugged. We went our separate way. He wasn't there to hurt me. He was there to be a friend.

I became infatuated with JT. I wanted to talk to him all the time on the phone. He shared this same interest with me. However, he had to leave for a few weeks. It was his dad's 70th Birthday Party. He had borrowed his brother's phone to keep in touch with me, since his was not getting good service.

I remember leaving him a voice-mail, because I could not get a hold of him.

"Hey JT. I just wanted to let you know that I was going to a baseball game with a… a "friend", and I would be unavailable to talk on the phone until I was done. Talk to you later. Hope you are having fun."

He knew I wasn't going to a baseball game with a "friend". I however, very much enjoyed sitting in club seats and riding in a BMW convertible with the top down. This guy, I had him listed in my phone as JM. It stood for Jeremy the Millionaire. That's fucked up to some. Not for me. I had to keep track of those guys I was dating.

All I could think about was JT. He was on my mind. I wasn't enjoying the date I was on. I was missing JT's words and his voice. His laughter. I WAS INFATUATED.

This evening I had to cut my date short with JM. I wanted to get home and talk to JT. I told him my babysitter had gotten sick and I needed to go. I never saw him again after this. He tried emailing and texting me. I had no desire or need for closure.

The second I closed the door to my car, I grabbed my phone and eagerly called JT.

"JT!"

"Hey!"

"Did you have a fun day?"

I ended up talking to him for a hour. Telling him more about me. Learning more about him. I was falling in love with this guy. I didn't even have sex. It was the normal and appropriate thing to do. What a concept. Waiting until you know it's right.

I had to make the move. I wanted this to be more than a friendship. I didn't want money. I wanted love. I wanted JT.

"Hey? I have a question to ask you."

"Shoot for it."

"I, umm, well I don't normally do things like this. This isn't in my nature."

"Your safe. Go for it."

"Okay, well, do you want to take this beyond a friendship? But here's the deal. NO ONE knows at the PD. NO ONE. 2nd we still get to see other people."

"Ha ha, nothing to lose. Well put. Yes. Let's do this."

I was so nervous, but excited! I wanted JT home. He was so far away. I wanted to sleep with him. I had to know what it was like to sleep with him! Okay, truth be told. I wasn't ever much for waiting. It was important to know if I enjoyed the "encounter" with the person, before I pursued the relation-ship any further.

We had planned a date for the fol-lowing Tuesday. JT came home the Monday before our first date and I in-vited him over. He told me he was ex-hausted from traveling and that he would see me for our date the following day. He was still on vacation days, so it worked out perfect for my days off.

I had been shot down. I was sad.
But that's okay. There was no reason I
needed him in person. We said good-
night, and I opened up my wine, and
watched TV.

KNOCK. KNOCK. KNOCK.

Who the fuck was at my door?
Probably Vincent. He always showed
up to my place unannounced. I had
hated that about him. He did that to
me while JT was out of town. He enjoyed his Millionaire lifestyle, but a free
couch to sleep on.

I had completely broke it off with
Vincent prior to my conversation with
JT. He had asked me to marry him.
He told me that if I married him, he'd
move me to Florida and hire a nanny
for my kids.

It was completely disturbing me. Here I had been searching for love in money, and it was staring me in my face. A two carat diamond perfect in every way, staring me in my face.

It wasn't the first or the second time I had been proposed to. It was actually Proposal Count Dracula Number 3. It was easy for me to turn him down.

He didn't know who the fuck I was. If he really knew who I was, he wouldn't have tried to relocate me. I was close to my family, and would for-ever remain close to them. They are my bear pack, my wolf pack.

Also, it was a thrill to me to be able to save lives. It was necessary for me to serve like that. I wasn't going to quit. I also hate the ocean. And there are rather large snakes in Florida. I HATE snakes! There was a lot more to the story but not a lot of time to tell it.

KNOCK. KNOCK. KNOCK.

I looked through the peep hole.

IT WAS JT!

He shocked me. I had told him where I lived once before. And since he's observant and well a COP, he found me. It wasn't hard.

I MADE LOVE to him that night.

The best love anyone could ever dream of. The kind of love that I was looking for. We were compatible. I trusted him. He was mine. I was never letting him go.

"JT?"

It wasn't in my nature to make the moves. I first asked him to date me, and now I am about to spill out my heart. I didn't want it to come across creepy or stalker-ish since all this went so quick. But I felt safe. Well for the time being.

"JT? Will you be exclusive with me? Will you be my boyfriend?"

The words uttered out of my mouth. He was discovering me. I was discovering him. I also mentioned to him that I needed a week to break it off with a few of the guys I was seeing.

OH.

That was difficult by the way. It was a long journey for me. But JT stuck by me. I told every guy how it was. Every single one of them. I was in a relationship.

We were inseparable. We made it work.

So essentially that was it, we had both done "marriage" before. We knew this feeling wasn't entirely new. And we knew we had a lot of shit to work on. BUT we were going to do it together. We shopped for the perfect house and blended our families. Everything came together quite perfectly.

"One must learn to love, and go though a good deal of suffering to get to it... and the journey is always toward the other soul."

— D.H. Lawrence

5

tracy

The PD stood 4 levels high. Dispatch was set on the 2nd level with the bullet hole windows (stated earlier- sorry I KNOW!) and the gym, break rooms, CSI, Evidence rooms were all on the basement pit level. The pit is where the 30 unused patrol cars were parked.

A LONG time ago maybe in the 80's, a disgruntled Police Officer started shooting his gun in the pit. No one was hurt. I always watched my back when I was heading in to work. Worrisome that there would be someone trying to take down a Cop.

During Graves, there was no one walking around. The PD Evidence Floor was always eerie, and quiet.

It was my turn to do a snack run. I gathered everyones money. I memorized everyones regulars. Jonie liked Diet Coke, I like Coke Zero, and so on. Cheetos, Snickers, Licorice, or whatever fatty foods went a long with the Diet.

I headed my way down through the stairwell and opened the door. The PD was newly built. Everything was new and clean. If I was lucky, I would run in to the creepy maintenance man that no one liked. I would smile at him, in hopes I wouldn't be a victim of another disgruntled employee shooting. These things happen YA KNOW? I would have considered giving him some candy, but wanted it all for myself.

The walls were painted grey. Not really quite sure why they couldn't paint it with happy colors, like yellow, orange, or cream even?

I opened the door and looked to the left. I heard a child's laughter. I was wondering if maybe one of the officer's had a child there. Occasionally officer's would have to bring kids in, and wait until Social Services arrived or a Victim Advocate.

NO child to be seen!

I proceeded to the vending machines. I heard tiny foot steps. I looked again and nothing.

WTF!

I calmed down my inner fears. It took me a second to gather my thoughts.

The laughter of the child again.

OKAY- this gives me the chills writing about it. Maybe this spirit or whatever needed me. I am in the process of learning more.

I collected my thoughts again and calmed myself down. I put the money in the vending machine and selected our yumminess. With all caffeine in hand, I headed my way back to dispatch.

I'd get my daily exercise in by climbing up the stairwell. I started to get worked up again over the noise. I'd made it up the first flight of steps. I found myself hurrying my way back into dispatch. I had to buzz my way back through two doors. I dispersed the drinks and sat back down.

At that moment I was working the data channel and not much of anything was going on. My co-worker Jonie could see I was upset.

"What's wrong? Did you run into a douche bag Cop?"

"There was a small child downstairs. I SWEAR- Jonie, I am not going crazy. It scared the hell out of me."

She laughed with amusement. And seemed entertained. But still sat completely intrigued.

She had worked for the department for over a decade. She wanted something more, and wanted to help people, so she came interviewed for dispatch and transferred. She told lot's of entertaining stories, and always made my day when I worked with her.

After many moments of silence Jonie began to spill her thoughts.

"Did you know there was an un-solved murder from1984? It was a young elementary girl?"

Jonie joked a lot, so I wasn't sure if this was a truth or not. This intrigued me. As bored as many dispatchers were, I started to access the old records. That failed since they were locked files. Only detectives and command staff could have access to them.

I researched as much as I could. So when all else fails, I turned to the in-ternet.

It was a joke around the PD that I was a Detective, mostly between JT's good buddies (Brian & Tommy) and I. I enjoyed history searches and learning new things. I also remembered a lot of details in regards to addresses and people, or events that occurred.

SO- without any schooling, and 9 years of 911 dispatching under my belt, I earned the nickname, Detective.

I utilized my passion for learning things. I had completed my nightly investigation.

Tracy Neef. Sweet baby JESUS. SHE is ME in reincarnation. Well not really, or maybe?

Tracy was a murdered THE EXACT same day I was born.

So with considerable suspicion and all my fears aside, I decided to welcome her sweet spirit. No guys, it's not my drugs.

RIP TRACY BABY DOLL. May some giving soul somewhere-somehow find the person who did this to you. This crime will be solved.

"Tracy Marie Neef, 7, was found dead near Barker Reservoir in Nederland in March 1984."

To the Psychic, the imagination is everything. The world is created through the imagination of God, and that same imaginative force is active in each of us.

—Henry Reed PH.D

It turns out that her red backpack she was wearing on the way to school and some other personal property items were found in Boulder County, Colorado. They remain in evidence.

A few days went on, and I did a snack run again. I made my way down the stairs. I didn't have fear so much as anticipation. I welcomed her laughter. And so, I heard it again. I saw a quick shadow as if she was playing peekaboo with me. I didn't say anything to her, but she knew I was there. I recognized her sweet spirit.

A couple weeks went on, and it was my turn to do the snack chore. As I treaded my way down the stairs, I saw an old red back laying in the hall. I quickly grabbed the snacks and the backpack. I ran my way up the stairs.

Jonie was sitting there in suspense and expectation.

I opened the backpack and in it were drawings, old clothing items, and random belongings from the early 80's.

HAHAHAHA!

Funny, funny, funny. I had been part of a cruel joke, planned by my boyfriend, and Jonie. I was a little more pissed then I led off to be. I felt manifested by her. I felt obligated to help find her murderer.

peace & bliss

JT was always the center of attention. He made people laugh. He was a conscious being. He was enlightening, uplifting, and illuminating. He was full of deep peace and bliss.

When I first heard his voice on the radio, my heart skipped a beat.

"Damn, what a nice voice. MMM-MM."

I could listen to that voice all night long.

Over many years, I had heard lots of voices. VOICES on the radio. SMILE.

I would get to know the voice and then see the face that stood behind it. The majority of times, it was a shock factor. Ugh. I'd prefer to envision what I wanted to envision. The good looking Fireman, or the Heroic Cop.

Being a cute dispatcher was a rarity. It's usually a joke that dispatchers are fat and sit behind a desk and eat all night. Well, to some extent that is true. It's also rarity to have time to exercise. It's a stationary job, and lasts for 8-12 hours at a time.

By the time any dispatcher gets off, it was time to zen out, eat, and then sleep. Depending on the type of calls that you took the shift before, or incidents that occurred with the Fire Department or Police Department, a heavy drink might need to be had.

I had my really good friends that I had worked with for years. I knew many of them well. I was transferred to the City just for a change of pace. It was higher in pay and better benefits.

Since the dispatch center was in the Police Department, we had frequent visitors. One of my friend's was a Sergeant, and I would make coffee for him. I knew how he took his coffee, a little cream and sugar.

Occasionally I would be busy, so he would just come up and make us all coffee. It was fun having all the different faces in. After all, the PD had over 200 of them. Men and WOmen. (WOooomen)

In dispatch we were frequented by visitors. Police Officers and Fire Fighters. I was usually the target of flirtation. But after the hard separation from my husband, I wanted to do something better for myself. I promised myself I would never date a COP.

I couldn't put myself through the heart ache of knowing they could die at the hands of another. I also didn't want to date people that I worked with. SO- essentially it become my promise to myself. No badges. However, a little flirtatious energy never hurt anyone.

On the day's I didn't have the kids, I'd fill the void by dating. I didn't have a lot of friends outside of law enforcement, or the fire world, so I'd become familiar with the world of online dating. It was so fun! TOXIC- but fun.

I will write another book on that another day.

I learned how to profile people based off status. For example, age, career, and income. I wanted to date men over 35 and wealthy. Millionaires, preferably. Judge me, I don't care. Call me a gold digger if you must, I was searching for an "investment" called love. I wanted to give my kids the best. I was eager for lifetime happiness.

I have learned now that MONEY is NOT happiness.

I found myself dating many guys. As stated earlier, 5 juggled at one time. I learned how to manage my time well. When my kids' dad had the children, and I wasn't working, I filled my time with fine dining, and lot's of sex. I had many adventures in my young age. I flew in a single airplane by a pilot I dated. I dated Lawyers who owned their own firms. I dated successful entrepreneurs, salesmen, realtors, architects and more.

This was completely unhealthy to my growth, but fun. Exasperating fun. I'd come in with my stories, and tell my girlfriends. They were envious of my ventures, but still guarded. They knew I had high expectations and a COP was not my perspective.

I was still dealing with the pain of divorce though. No one wants their family split up. It was best for the me and the kids to be away from our constant arguments. So I had run from the pain inside me. I worked, I hardly ate, I tanned, I made myself so called beautiful. Beautiful for someone. Not myself.

Another random officer came in the room. He was so loud! I slid myself down in the chair and hid behind my desk so I didn't have to get to know someone else that I didn't need to. He was hyper, and hilarious. I was completely unamused.

I could tell he was attempting to get my attention, but I didn't care. It wasn't flattering. On certain days I'd entertain the fact that most 5-O liked me. But that particular day I wasn't. I didn't budge from my seat or turn around. Heck, I had five guys at that moment that I had enjoyed "hanging" out with. These were men I didn't have to talk about death, chaos, and fucked up shit.

I wanted my mind off of work. I came to work, and I left that shit in the chair. I didn't want to bring it home with me. I learned that trick after 3 miserable years of dispatching.

THANK GOD! He left.

I received a request notification on my cell phone from a networking site moments later. I didn't recognize the person, and I turned to my co-worker and asked who it was. He quickly lit up and told me it was Officer Walker.

"You know, the guy that was just in here!?"

Well I didn't know, because I hadn't looked. I didn't care. I accepted the friend request and moved on. After all, it's the courteous thing to do. Dysfunctional, but courteous right?

If he thought I was entertaining his existence by letting him be privy to my page and pictures, then he had something coming to him.

april fools

On April 1st, 2010, I had called in sick to work because I had been feeling well, SICK. After pushing fluids, and eating some popsicles that my sister bought me, I quickly recovered.

Hmm, must have been stress.

One of my millionaire boyfriends I had been dating at the time lived in Vail. Vincent. The guy I had thought was knocking on the door earlier.

He called me and told me I should drive up because there was a concert that evening. It was a **DJ** that was performing exclusively and he had tickets.

I was eager to take the drive. It took me under two hours to get there. It was relaxing for me to speed around the mountains. I quickly packed my bag, showered, and got ready.

It was warm for an April day in Colorado. I put on some leggings, a cute little dress, and some flip flops. My toes were painted pink! I was 25 and loving it! I felt alive for the first time in my life.

Well other than my poisonous career.

This same boyfriend had taken me to Vegas for my Birthday a month before. I liked the thrill of money. He'd spend $30,000 in one sitting.

He liked me because I wasn't the average gold digger. I didn't ask for him to buy me things, although he did. I didn't really even need the money. Just the adventures. The freedom from my thoughts. What went from finding financial freedom in men to negligence and avoidance of myself.

He taught me how to play Black-Jack. I was lucky! I one $900 bucks. He started to get really pushy though, so I backed off.

I didn't like talking to guys when I had my kids, and hardly let them meet anyone. I wasn't the average clingy girlfriend. Mostly because I didn't care. I dated multiple guys to get just what I wanted out of each one individually. Then on to the next.

I just wanted to date and have sex at their expense. Not mine.

I jumped in my little black 9-3 Saab Turbo, and off for some therapy. Therapy from my world of hate that intoxicated me. It once was love, but quickly turned in to hate.

It was a very warm sunny Colorado day. The sun was out so I opened the sunroof. I listened to music and cruised the mountains. It usually took me about 1.5 hours to get to Vail from where I lived.

I hit Eisenhower Tunnel which meant I didn't have much time until I got to Vail, and it slowly started to snow. I was bummed since I wasn't dressed accordingly for the weather. I was still cruising. The weather was getting worse and was not in my favor.

I had slowed down. I was maybe going 30 miles per hour. I was paying close attention to the conditions. My car was awesome in the snow, it had a winter feature!

I quickly hit the winter road conditions button and continued to cruise. I loved snow driving. I was great at it- since I had been driving in it since I was 16.

I quickly drew near to a blind corner. I slowed WAY down. There were several cars stopped and several that had crashed.

"Oh FUCK!"

I had to figure out what to do. I couldn't stop… I couldn't slow down. I was terrified! It was a nightmare that had come true. Death awaits. I stared at it straight in the face.

I slowed the engine down by putting it into 2nd gear, I quickly changed to first. I was dodging cars. Up ahead appeared to be a large semi truck truck, jackknifed. I was about to go under it and decapitate myself.

I knew I had to crash. I quickly turned my wheels fast as I could, much like a video game and hit the back of a Red SUV.

My car continued to slide.

I felt like I was going 30 MPH since this was all down hill. There was snow everywhere.

Complete chaos.

I crashed and I crashed hard.

I protected my face with my arm, which later I learned was not the best to do.

Glass flew everywhere!

I was in so much pain. I closed my eyes, and lost consciousness. Later I had learned that I was hit by several vehicles. 8, I believe.

I don't really know how much time had gone by. I had been unconscious for quite awhile and finally I woke up. I was terrified. It still snowing.

My door began to open up.

A blonde, blue eyed guy opened my door. He was dressed for the weather. Smart, very intelligent. Winter Man.

"Hey guys over here, there is some-one in here in this Saab!"

He put his coat on me. He grabbed my bag from the back and helped put my warmer shoes on. He told me go wait in his car.

He did not crash. He was able to pull off the road. His car was a little four door, blue Volvo. It was so warm. He offered me a cigarette. I shook my head no.

He told me that he was here for me and would help me get my belongings. We exchanged numbers.

I was in so much pain. Something was wrong with my arm. The fire department took forever to get there. Maybe a little over a hour.

I had to hike down the mountain next to a girl on a stretcher. One of the bitches that hit me. It wasn't her fault. I did the same thing too.

There were six people in the ambulance riding with me. All complaining of one thing or another. This lady in the ambulance put some lavender oil on me. She said it would calm me down. It most certainly did.

I was 5 minutes from Vail.

5 MINUTES??? Yeah right. Well, it should have been. The ambulance ride took forever!

I finally had service on my cell phone, so I called my sister. I told her I had been in a bad accident. She thought I was kidding since it was April 1st.

"Haha April Fools!"

I could hear how pissed she was through the phone. It took me a moment to speak.

"Tina, I am not kidding."

She was so pissed. After all, that morning she had brought me all the necessities to recover from what could have been the flu or STRESS.

I later called my Vail boyfriend. He had met me at the hospital, along with Winter Man. Oh boy, did that piss him off. I was quickly triaged since there were a multitude of patients coming in.

I had so much swelling on my arm, that they could not determine if there was a break or not. They wrapped my arm in a sling, treated my burns from the air bag, and released me. My boyfriend and I went on our way.

Oh, and drugs, lot's of good drugs.

I couldn't believe it happened to me. I had to call work. Completely ashamed. I had explained to them what had happened. I was stuck in Vail for a few day's until the weather cleared.

I just wanted to be home.

We still had went out that night, heavily medicated. Guys would bump into my sling at the bar. It hurt. My boyfriend yelled and told them he was going to sue them if they'd hurt me. I guess that is what rich people do? Just kidding.

The weather cleared and we finally made our route home. The roads were terrible. I couldn't look. I was fearful of snow. I was fearful of cars. I was fearful of Vinnie.

I laid the seat back and tried to sleep. I never ever ever wanted to go back to Vail. Never again.

I quickly recovered and was ready to get back to work. I decided that this was God's way or the Universe's way

of telling me to get my shit together.
So I did. I did a lot of self healing.

At that time of my life, a lot of self healing was taking time to be alone. To reflect on my life. Be the best mom I could be. I was tired, sad, depressed, and lonely. Work was an outlet for me. As much as I have expressed my hate for it, I was addicted to it. Hearing other people's problems made it easier to deal with my own.

ego

"911, What's the address of your emergency?"

"Help me, help me, help me!"

"Ma'am, I need you to calm down so I can get help to you, Okay? What's the address of your emergency?"

This woman kept screaming, I had to use every calming technique that I knew.

"My son is hanging, he's hanging, he's dead."

I never knew who or what was going to be on the other end. It could be something as petty as a fear of bugs, to the extreme of multiple shootings. Whatever came in, I had to be prepared. These people needed me.

The officers needed me, the firefighters needed me, my coworkers needed me, my kids needed me. I didn't have time right now to deal with anyone else needing me. After all, I was hurting. I was hurting deep inside.

A few months past, I continued to self reflect. To become a better employee and a better mother. I pushed out anyone who wanted to cause harm to me. I was recovering from a difficult childhood, a very pushy in the face religious experience, and recovering from the death of all the people I was surrounded by during my marriage. They didn't really die, but it felt like it to me. I was in no place to date.

You cannot make the egoless state into a future goal and then work toward it. All you get is more dissatisfaction, more inner conflict, because it will always seem that you have not arrived yet, have not "attained" that state yet. When freedom from ego is your goal for the future, you give yourself more time, and more time means more ego.

—Eckhart Tolle

My first day back to work after the

 Vail Accident-

In walked a very tall Sergeant. I knew a lot of gossipy shit about this man, mostly stuff from working with the police department for over 9 years. He was gorgeous!

I was definitely attracted to him.

I loved the way he looked at me when he walked in the room. He was a cocky asshole. But I liked that. He knew he was attractive.

At this time, I was working a day shift position. It was slow, and there were a lot of people working. This allowed me to chat with him at my dispatch pod. pod = office cubicle

There were supervisors and command staff walking in an out. We knew how to make the conversation look appropriate. Derek decided to target my accident as a way to get to know me a little more.

I was terribly naive.

Wow, what a nice guy… He wants to try to help me. He asked me for my number, and I gave it to him.

DUMB. D-U-M. DUM.

A text message came through immediately. I was excited and checked it. After all, even with a cast on, I looked cute. I still got it!

"Let's get together tonight at this little tavern over at the Braeburn."

It's not a place that is frequented by people we know.   This will work out perfect!

Conveniently, I was open and available. Anything to spend an evening with this sexy guy. BUT not getting in a relationship with him, nor getting in bed. Absolutely not. NOPE. NOPE. Sticking to rich guys and self healing.

I arrived a little late. The Tavern was dark, but decorated to look like an old Irish Pub. It had a "coffee shop" atmosphere to it. I walked in, and all eyes were on me. There were no women in site with exception of the wait staff. They were not as cute as me.

Please for the life of me, don't think I walk around strutting my stuff. I just have learned my awesome attributes! I could use them to get the things I wanted.

If you are good looking, it's okay to admit it to yourself. To look in the mirror and say, hey, damn, SEXY TIME! VERY NICE. I LIKE. I got it going on. Momma is hot.

Just kidding around.

Back to tall-handsome Sergeant…

Derek was sitting there at the bar. He probably had two beers down. He grabbed the waitress immediately and got me a Blue Moon with a slice of orange.

I gave Derek a disgusted and annoyed face. I told him not to order that shit for me. I was actually in the mood for a Jack and Coke. Beer made me bloat. I'm not a prissy bitch that has to be catered to. IN FACT, I had no means of dating this guy. This "meeting" was supposed to be professional.

I WAS NOT going to be another target, or a tight pussy for him to fuck. Except, I was curious and kinda wanted to see his penis. I knew he had big hands. He was 6' 6. He clearly had to have a large penis!

So what did I do? I drank the blue moon. He talked to me about my considerations on suing over the accident.

It never even occurred to me that my freak accident was something I could sue over. I needed too though. After all, I was billed for the entire ambulance ride. What happened was not my fault. It was all because of the jack knifed semi.

WELL ultimately it was the universes way of telling me to stop sabotaging my life.

I also had a jack and coke and had sat long enough to finally leave. I thanked Derek for meeting me and helping me. That was painless.

Derek insisted on paying. To set the record straight, I advised him that this was a professional meeting and let him pay. It wasn't an expensive evening after all.

Derek walked me out to my car. He insisted on coming over to my house. He told me that he had an awesome bottle of wine in his car and he was waiting for the right moment to pop it open.

Derek insisted that he wanted to celebrate my return to work and wanted to talk to me about a topic at had briefly brought up to him.

I had mentioned to him that I wanted to write a book. Well as a matter of fact, Derek's sister was a famous author! thor!

For privacy reasons, I cannot tell you who this person is. But I will say, I had **NO IDEA** that he was **HER** sister. I loved this author. I was beyond enthused. I was ecstatic on the inside.

"If you bring the wine, you can come over! I can't wait to hear all about this!"

My house was 5 quick minutes south of the Tavern. Drive time, that is. I was elated that he was coming over. I hoped that my house was clean. Fuck it, who cared.

We popped open the bottle of wine.

This was fine wine, I had thought to myself. Maybe a $400.00 bottle of wine? I didn't want him to think that I was impressed or had known anything about wine. I was a twenty somethings dispatcher.

I however had learned quite a bit about wine when I was out dating "millionaires". The VINO dates I had been on were not cheap. Millionaires never ever drink cheap wine. Well in my personal experience that is.

I briskly searched for my cheap ass wine glasses.

Derek poured the wine. I picked up my glass. I took a deep inhale. I waited for the final escape of the bubbles.

I took another deep breath and another deep inhale. It was bold, rich and complex. I sipped it. I finished it. I regained depth and dimension.

Drink now through this euphoria.

DRINK DRINK DRINK.

"Another glass please!"

Derek was pleased that I was enjoying the fine wine.

Of course one thing led to the other. We succumbed to our sexual tension in my dark, messy room. He had no hair on his body, and was gorgeous.

I had later described him to my complexed and distanced best friend, Abbie.

"He's a stallion."

Derek, The Stallion.

Haha! I laugh now. But Derek was huge. The biggest cock I had ever had. Go big, or go home.

GOOOO HOME! OUCH!

I will never, never, never, EVER, EvEr, EVER, go there again. An elephant cock.

A STALLION.

NOPE, never, EVER want anyone to find out about that.

So the secret had been told, when shortly after that traumatic event, I met MY LOVER and told him about Derek at coffee.

JT MY HEART SONG.

THE MAN I COULD AND WILL NEVER ALLOW TO DIE, before me that is.

hero in a cape

JT. He intoxicates me, yet poisons me. VENOM. He captivates me.

HE DID. Why? Why?

WHY the FUCK?

GOD, UNIVERSE. Why did you do this to me.

This sure is a fucked up way for you to show your control.

DON'T TAKE HIM AWAY FROM ME. I WILL HATE YOU FOREVER.

We need him. People need him. Children need him. My hero. A man with a cape. MY hero.

> "Left behind the perfect crime, echoes swell, then SUBSIDE."
>
> — Author Unkown

Why is it that accidents are so GRUESOME?

Full of blood splattered brain matter all over the highway. Heads decapitated. People screaming.

Infant heads stuck in the front windshield, while the body remains secure in the car seat. ALL because DRUNK mom and dad clearly were not supposed to drive. Yes GRUESOME.

I still think of you and all the shit you put me through, JT.

My lover.

MY HEART SONG.

My usually routine once I arrive at work, is to start by unlocking my locker. The locker is in the dispatch break room. Their really wasn't ever a "real" break allowed.

The manager of the call center at the time, wanted the radio traffic of both Fire, and Police, up. It was audible, and not only was I taking a break, but I had to listen to both agencies! We were not allowed to leave the PD either. No food runs, so the officer's on duty would grab us lunch.

I arrived at work the beginning of May about one week from my one night stand with The Stallion of a Sergeant. I hadn't run into him since. I absolutely DID NOT want to.

PLEASE, please, NEVER run into him.

I unlocked my locker and grabbed my bag. My bag consisted of my headphones, and work folders. I usually kept a box of oatmeal in my locker in case I needed a quick fix.

I opened the door to dispatch from the break room with my proxy card.

BEEP.

UNLOCKED.

Oh MAN.

That feeling of walking in the door.

It was neither good energy or bad energy.

I routinely made a new batch of coffee. You never know how old or how stale a dispatch pot of coffee could be.

I heated my oatmeal up.

What the hell do we have here?

I looked amongst all of my un-opened mail- directly on the top- lay a package. It wasn't my birthday? It wasn't any special occasion. It was just another day.

The package was neatly wrapped in brown paper. Similar to a brown paper bag from the grocery store, but nicer. On top of the wrapped package was a pink bow, intricately placed in the center.

I melted, I wondered what it was. I took it to my desk. I was assigned to the Fire Channel.

I LOVED dispatching Fire. It was an adrenaline rush. My calm voice would be heard in every Fire Station in the city.

EMERGENCY EMERGENCY.

BIG RED TRUCK EMER-GENCY.

"FIRE UNIT 700, standby for a tone on a STRUCTURE FIRE."

I set my mouse on FIRE CALL ALL Tab. If I didn't tone it perfectly-it would mean an Engine wouldn't get their pages or tones in the department for the call. NO BUENO.

"FIRE UNIT 700, STATION 1 as primary- RESPOND on a Structure Fire at 9561 East Colorado Summit Pkwy."

They had 1 minute to the T to ac-knowledge the tones. I had to call over the radio to make sure units were enroute. Arrival time needed to be less than 3 minutes for the first Engine.

LOUD FIRE TONES

"ENG72, ENG73, ENG74, ENG75, BC71, ENG31, MEDIC71, and MED31- RESPOND on a STRUCTURE FIRE at 9561 E Colorado Summit Pkwy."

ROLL CALL TIME!

I loved hearing the voices of the fire fighters. Depending on the time of the night, they were either really grumpy, or very excited. ALSO- it depends on how long of a shift they had left.

"Engine72 EN-ROUTE"

Sometimes if the traffic (a dispatch term for verbiage aired over the radio) was unreadable- I would be able to look at my radio screen and see which radio unit popped up. The radios were all programmed with the designator.

For example, 3Tom64's radio belonged to Officer O'Connor. And ENG71, was the radio installed in Engine71. I always made duty employees (FIRE, MEDICAL, POLICE) repeat their radio traffic. I have heard way to many stories of Officer's needed help, and no one prompted and confirmed traffic. Even if a unit popped up on my radio screen, and traffic did not come across, I would still ask if they were Code 4.

Code 4 meant that they were of good status or A-OKAY. or TEN-FOUR. We did not use 10 Code with the city.

I continued through the rest of the tone, and sent all units.

All units had arrived.

After all the times and all the dis-patch/police/fire jargon ensued- I took a deep breath. I would patiently wait for the next big thing to come. Or not patiently wait. Sometimes it would happen all over again immediately.

Never a dull moment when you have lives to save.

I loved "BIG THINGS" or any-thing that would make my heart beat. I loved Adrenaline rushes! I loved the feeling of getting butterflies in my stomach. It always made the shift go by faster.

I was constantly reminded of the time. When clearing the air- you'd time stamp.

2311.

I loved ending my shift. This meant I was closer to seeing my baby! My babies! And MY BED!

911.

Always drama, always something, always murder, always medical responses, always nursing home calls, always misdials, call backs, suicides, accidents, fires, domestic violences, disturbances, alarms, false alarms, holdups, robberies, burglaries, civil issues, family disturbances, shootings, sex assaults, I/P (in progress), J/O (just occurred less than 15 minutes), or COLD calls. I am sure you get the point.

911 is EVERYTHING to everyone.

the gift

I looked down, and was quickly reminded of my gift.

OH YEAH! MY GIFT! YAY!

I once received a very stalker like gift from a millionaire architect I had dated for a few months. His name was Lonnie.

I must drift off, and tell you this story.

Lonnie was hilarious! He was great energy when I had found him on a dating website. I was an active member and very much enjoyed profiling people, and looking at pictures.

My profile red something like this.

Single Mother, very involved in my children's lives. They are my priority, and no you may not meet them.

I am looking for a potential loving relationship.

I very much enjoy a night out, serious relationships, casual relations, or exotic night out. I do not enjoy movies on the first date because I want to get to know you!

Please do not wink at me, or send me a message if you have any pictures on your profile of your stupid accomplishments.

-I caught my biggest fish or look at me I shot a fox-

OR your almost naked body.

Don't WINK if you have pictures of things like MAN HAIR-THE TRAIL to YOUR TAIL or your little muscles, your big muscles, or anything along those lines.

I enjoy a nice coffee date, dinner date, VINO date, or whatever adventures or heroic things we my venture.

Lonnie's pictures were of him against a S.W.A.T. UNIT, with his hands crossed in a manner as if he was under arrest. He clearly wasn't. Hmmm, he thought he was a fun-neeee guy was he? It had humored me.

The next picture was of him in the driver's seat of a Red Porsche SUV. It was a side profile which complimented his lightly feather spiked, short blonde hair. He had nice sporty black sunglasses on. The sun shined through the slightly cracked tinted drivers side window. The sun effect, photo editing, all made me see a little beauty in this guy.

I learned from experience, not to invest a lot of time, or conversation on a stranger. I also learned to not fear a meet with this stranger. A lot of my friends were worrisome over the possibility that I could kidnapped, drug raped, or burned on a tree by gangsters. But the rarity of this actually occurring via a paid membership only dating website was slim to none. Oh trust me, I have heard all the horror stories.

No fear, however, meeting the "interested party" was always in a very public spot. They were never allowed to come to my home. A meet usually occurred after a few emails.

Back to Vinnie from Vail, his email read, "Let's go out for VINO! Text me the date, and I will make arrangements to come down."

I texted him immediately after looking through his profile. Independent Stock Management, made some very successful investments. I am a spontaneous, single 40 year old. I am always looking for a good time! I enjoy traveling, fine dining, and nights on the couch with our favorite movie on.

Lonnie on the other hand, showed a little more emotional interest in me. We had emailed only because our work schedules did not compliment our meetings. After several weeks of nice text messages, email exchanges, and phone conversations, we had a meeting ground planned. FINALLY.

We had learned that we both had the same coffee order at "everyones favorite" coffee shop. The logo is of a green mermaid.

*Hint *Hint *Wink *Wink.

We had mutually agreed on the location of the meet or date(whatever you would like to call it). The local bookstore "green logo" also had the favorite coffee shop inside. We called each other upon our arrival. We saw each other through the windshields of our parked cars. We agreed to meet at the front of the store and hung up.

Our eyes locked onto each other. I gave a quick pretentious smile, and slowly walked up to him.

It was dark, and a little bit nippy outside. There were glimmering, wet, smaller snowflakes that had drifted slowly down to the ground. I loved how my favorite houndstooth black and white, slightly snug, fashion-eeee jacket looked on me. A Nordstrom Rack find. I wore tight jeans, which were purchased by another guy that had asked me to marry him.

That's a whole-nuth-er story.

Oh, and I can't forget my black UGGS! I had a cute black felt hat on. My eyes were outlined in black eye liner. I spritzed a lightly scented perfume on me, which was also another gift from someone else.

I loved free gifts, or surprise shopping trips to buy whatever I wanted.

My first instinct, was instantaneous. HE was going to be "just" another guy that would fall in love with me.

He reached for a hug, and expressed his joy over finally meeting me. He had a sensual scent that radiated from his expensive leather jacket. He was wearing jeans, a nice dress shirt tucked is jeans. A rugged, burnt brown mplimented his very fit waistline. 'gh anticipations to learn more about this guy over #coffee, #cologne #perfumem, #alldolledup, #coffeefor-daze, #blinddatehorrorstories.

He was so extremely nervous. Poor guy, I guess I had to bust out some of my all knowing calming techniques. Oh joy. Oh boy.

It ended up turning into several more dates, and his request for me to be exclusive. We actually had a lot in common, and I enjoyed his many interests. He was an architect, and had built his own hugenormous house.

Lonnie enjoyed beer, decorating, hanging with his children, and me. He was very needy, and wanted to know my every thought. The few dates turned in to his request for me to move in. He had even went shopping for me clothing, and makeup, and toiletries fo his house. He was suffocating me, so I played him along to get nice things. After a few months, I had broke it off via text message.

Messed up, I know. I already have made my peace with my bad Karmic energy seeds I planted.

The break up message quickly turned to stalking mannerisms, harassing emails, and flower deliveries to work.

I had arrived home from work. I had gone in for an overtime shift of a few hours near Christmas. I unlocked my door, only to find a large array of intricately decorated gifts. Each gift was individually labeled. There also sat an expensive bouquet of Christmas oriented flowers. There layer a white envelope, tucked amongst the greenery.

It was a card. To the left was a man's scarf, completely unfamiliar.

Who the fuck had broke into my house?

I quickly cleared my house, and had my phone in hand. I was prepared to dial 911. There was no evidence of a break in. However, I had left my favorite jacket with a spare key at Lonnie's house. FUCK.

All of the gifts were from Lonnie. They were all very thoughtful and tastefully selected gifts. There were many boutique shop purchases. From a cloth baby dolls, stuffed animals, and other toys for my children to an iPad, a very stuffed Vintage Louis Vuitton Wallet which was compliment by a cute trendy makeup bag stuffed with several

$100 BILLS. $3,000 to the exact amount.

I tore open the card. Tastefully chosen card. I opened the inside and it were the following words…

*ENJOY IT ALL, YOU CAN HAVE ALL THIS AND MORE, JUST CALL ME, AND I WILL BE THERE.

MERRY JOLLY HOLIDAYS, WISH YOU WERE WITH ME NOW, L.*

"Ugh." I gasped.

I quickly dialed up a good friend of mine. He conveniently was in law enforcement.

Woot. Gotta utilize your resources!

He got rid of the problem. The big problem, L.

Threats? Exchanges of gentleman to gentleman words? Who knows? He's gone. A little block block from Facebook, and extra blocked from my cell phone. No texts or calls allowed from his number.

Flirtation, casual sex, and dates with strangers can lead to freak things. FrEaK occurrences, unwanted universal dimensional placements, and treading amongst dangerous territory of the heart.

I broke his heart. I broke his creepy heart.

Lesson learned. Moved on.

BACK TO THE PACKAGE

OpeN SeSaMe!!!

A BOOK. Not just ANY BOOK, a title and an author that was Déjà Vu for me. I tried to open the gift without entertaining all of my co-workers.

After all, they ought to be use to all the random gifts us "cute dispatchers" frequently received within the emergency responders world of men. 100's of men with a God complex.

These men would regularly cheat on their wives with dispatchers and give us gifts. Yep, it's a real world, real life epidemic.

Once upon a time, there was an inner departmental hot love affair going on. The dispatcher girlfriend murdered her police commander boyfriend. Or something like that. Who would have thought the kind of drama that comes from a PD. I hear the firefighters do it too!

Oh MY!

It should clearly be illegal. The operation of any 911 Emergency Center should be illegal. Murder, affairs, emotional affairs, hot sex in patrol cars, hot sex on patrol cars... OH- I must make a list of things to do.

*THE MUST DO LIST WHILE HAV-
ING A LOVE AFFAIR WITH A COP*

1. Sex in a field a little outside of
    the City.

2. Sex in vacant houses.

3. Sex inside the dispatchers large
    SUV, parked right in the view of
    the outside security cameras, mon-
    itored at the supervisors station.
    This SUV must be parked next to
    the empty patrol car. (TRUE
    EVENT).

4. During an assigned ride-a-long,
    please RIDE ON.

5. Describe a sexual experience
    between the two of you in extreme
    depth over court recorded phone
    calls, or even better, describe it
    over recorded and closely moni-
    tored MDT messages. (TRUE
    EVENT also by the same person

who successfully completed step
number 3 above.)

*THE MUST DO LIST WHILE HAV-
ING A LOVE LOVE AFFAIR WITH A
FIRE FIGHTER*

1. Sex on top of the sofa, in the
   QUIET room. The #1 mission with-
   in this task is- YOU MUST BE QUI-
   ET.

2. During an assigned ride-a-long,
   YOU MUST RIDE ON.

3. Sex in a big red truck.

4. Sex on a big red truck.

5. Picture messages sent between
   the two of you, while you work,
   while he works. Especially if he is
   the feature of a month in the Year-
   ly Firefighter Calendar.

I continued to investigate the thoughtful gift.

Derek. Of course. The gift was from Derek.

The story begins when you open the cover of a book.

I opened the cover of the book. Signed by the author herself.

"For a true princess

Samantha

—Love..."

"Oh Almighty God,

Whose Great Power And Eternal Wisdom
Embraces The Universe,

Watch Over All Policemen and Law Enforcement Officers.

Protect Them From Harm In The Perfor-
mance Of Their Duty

To Stop Crime, Robberies, Riots And Vio-
lence.

We Pray, Help Them Keep Our Streets, And
Homes Safe Day And Night.

We Recommend Them To Your Loving Care

Because Their Duty Is Dangerous.

Grant Them Your Unending Strength And

Courage In Their Daily Assignments.

Dear God, Protect These Brave Men,

Grant Them Your Almighty Protection,

Unite Them Safely With Their Families

After Duty Has Ended.

AMEN."~Author Unkown

the heart beat

Close your eyes. Imagine with me for just a moment. Inhale. Exhale. Feel your heart beat.

The heart beats.

It pumps blood.

I can feel this in my head. My heart beat is so rapid, my deep fear, it has come true. I am having a heart attack. I slowly slip away. I lose my mind in something I did not want to see. This was not a fantasy. I heard you die.

heart

/härt/

noun

1. a hollow muscular organ that pumps the blood through the circulatory system by rhythmic contraction and dilation. In vertebrates there may be up to four chambers (as in humans), with two atria and two ventricles.

2. the central or innermost part of something.

verb/informal

1. like very much; love.

How could I have been so lucky? I found you. I didn't deserve you. You broke the code to my heart. I could not be more intoxicated by you, my crazy, lover.

There was not a silent moment that evening, the evening I lost you.

I titled this book Morbid Lovers, for my lover, the only one who knows the real me. I didn't know what you saw in me. I was so sure you would have split and run.

Run rabbit, run.

It was a very dark twisted fantasy. A quick duality of events, welcomed to the inner workings of the world's mind. Dark and twisted. Twisted and dark. I am losing my breath. This is reality.

My lover had already gone to work. I had gone in a few hours early. I got to work the patrol channel. Which meant I got to see my lover before he hit the street.

I took the elevator from dispatch to the basement level of the PD. I took a left, and did the casual gravitation into a room full of Police Officers, ready to get their last shift in before their day's off. This particular swing shift consisted of the crew.

The crew that will forever be brothers and sisters in blue. They describe the blue line as a family crest. At times it can be stronger than blood. I knew the routine. Briefing started at a prompt 2215.

The north Sgt. "3T20" gave his spiel. Then the south Sgt. "3T21" gave his speech. Everyone was excited to have me on the radio. The flow was better when there was a senior dispatcher on shift. I had my fair share of crazy happen to me on the radio.

The usual shift was on. GiGi (JT went to the in house academy with her), she was the little sister on the shift. She got her shit done and was good at it. She was bitter sweet. She had her dark brown hair pulled up in a pony tail.

She was considered cute to many. She had tan skin for the winter months, and perfectly white teeth. She was rough, tough, but quite simple. I had gotten to know her pretty well. I trusted my lover's life in her hands.

Tommy, stood almost "stallion" tall. He was strong. He had shot a guy while I was working the 911 call on the line. We had that night in common. I loved Tommy. JT loved Tommy. GiGi loved Tommy. Then there was Brian. All best friends. All of them, close, so very close. Brian had property North of the city. He had a shooting range all set up for the 5-O to target shoot. HE would also have some amazing parties!

A mind is like a parachute. It doesn't work if it is not open.
— Frank Zappa

RED NECK HILLBILLY PARTY 5-1- 5-O DID Someone Call the PO PO?

JT and I would grab Oscar Blues beer, and our mutually favorite Whiskey. BULLEIT. Smooth, straight, satisfying.

BUZZED.

JT wasn't rednecked up enough for Brian's and I. We insisted on cutting JT's already torn jeans in to shorts.

Little did JT know; we had an agenda. Success! We talked JT into taking his pants off and waiting for his altered more red necked pair of shorts!

"HAHAHAHA!"

"Girls! This isn't good!", JT yelled.

We had a plan. Laughter continued to break out between us. We had converted JT's Redneck Pants into Red Neck Short Shorts. Who was gonna where short shorts?

JT was going to wear and ROCK short shorts.

He was crazy and spontaneous that night. I fell more in love with him that night, then ever before.

Laughter quickly spread at the party. He was always the life of the party. It has often been said, "The party doesn't start until Walkez arrives!".

I walked around the Bon Fire, singing, and strumming his guitar. My girlfriends/cute dispatcher coworkers had been invited to come to the party. JT found Jessica. Jessica had perfect skin, and a perfect smile. Her smile, and bright teeth complimented her light blue eyes. She was a few years younger than I, but we shared mutual interests, and similar morbid thoughts. She was also a very cute dispatcher.

JT danced and sang to Jessica, making her laugh immensely. His ball was showing through the hole in his pants.

OH MY GOSH.

"Put your balls away BABE!"

Laughter filled the chill air. Every one, every single one had eyes on JT. They engaged in his energy. It was filling. He had a place in everybody's hearts.

We had it made.

.911.

In between dispatching calls, or taking 911 calls, or whenever a quiet moment, I would look at my phone. I was always eager, waiting for JT's words to affirm me. I loved sending him text messages too. Our messaging would get us through the night, and kept us close.

I slipped into a daydream about JT.

I started to drift back into the morning when I felt the loss of him. The loss of my heart song.

That morning I had cuddled up against JT. We held on to each other.

He held me against his chest. I lost sight of myself, and became one with him. I closed my eyes, my ears, and my mind.   I made a connection with his inner dimension.

This was so DIVINE.

"JT?"

"Yeah baby? What's wrong baby? Why are you crying? Don't cry"

JT displayed sincere concern as he pulled me with force into his chest.

I had just come undone. I orgasmed and experienced closeness with him.

ONENESS.

Closeness. And it was out of my hands.

That's my man.

JT was intense. I was drowning in the moment. We CAME undone together. I was completely addicted to his touch. His tender grasp, and gentle strokes against my thighs. My hips. His hips.

We CAME at the same time.

This feeling brought up and intense emotion. Hormones maybe? Or just an open heart.

I still hate reliving that moment.

It was the first time, I had felt, the thought of my love dying. Of losing it all. The risk of the job. Someone shooting him, or another incident occurring. I cried with the misery in my mind.

I could lose him.

This man, who has my heart, could be gone at the hands of another.

Was this something I could do?

A total of 1,501 law enforcement officers died in the line of duty during the past 10 years, an average of one death every 58 hours or 150 per year.

On average, over the last decade, there have been 58,261 assaults against law enforcement each year, resulting in 15,658 injuries

BURY US ALIVE.

CRAP- I have to go to briefing! I escaped from my daydream and jumped into the elevator and made my way in to briefing.

I was ready for the shift. One time, I had a train vs. pedestrian accident, multiple gun shot victims from a bar fight gone bad, and a plane crash all in one shift when I worked patrol radio!

I considered myself well educated in the career, and well experienced none the less.

Time for hell.

Time for another night of adrenaline dumping.

Briefing broke up. I met my lover outside for a quick kiss in the pit. I watched him pack his patrol car, and drive away. He was in God's hands. Nothing I could do.

He was pain free. Damage free.

My world split in two, I can't do it without you. I knew something was

going to happen. Something was stabbing me in the gut.

What a curse. Maybe it was the psychic in me? Maybe Baby Doll Tracy
was telling me?

I remembered the moment from
that morning again. The feeling of my
tears crashing against his chest as he
pulled me closer, and closer.

JTW. I will not live without you. I
can't live without you. You are perfect
for me. You are the only person who
could tame my wild heart.

I entered dispatch. Plugged in.
Gathered my thoughts. I was ready,
ready for anything.

Saturday, January 29th, 2011 wasn't just a normal shift. The streets were crazy. There was no escape. I couldn't get enough Cops to cover the street. I already had 50+ on the streets.

T=TOM

Please read as 3TOM63. Proper designator radio terminology.

DISTI=Disturbance

I/P = In Progress

3T74=GiGi

3T64=JT

3T21= Max Dano

3T20= Cash Evan

3T62= Brian

3T72= Tommy

I selected the radio transmit button using the radio screen.

"3T64, 3T74 to cover on a DISTI/ I/P 100th/York."

"3T64, en-route." GiGi advised over the radio. Her voice was soft but firm.

My baby. The sound of his voice made me so happy. So protected. I was high off of his devotion.

I immediately forgot about my inner fears of something happened to JT.

"3T74- EN-ROUTE- go ahead."

"3T64- 3T74 as a pair on a DISTI in the area of 100th/York. The RP called and advised the there was an active physical disturbance between an unknown male, and female."

"BREAK."

"3T62- 3T72 as a pair on a suspicious party."

"3T62- Go."

Tommy liked to sound cocky and strong on the radio.

"3T72."

Brian was always direct and to the point.

"RP advised the neighbor saw a black male walking around the club house at 2100 West."

Everyone knew exactly what trailer park 2100 was. A very problematic trailer park.

"2T61- Traffic!"

"2-61 go ahead."

2T61 was a swing shift car. Him yelling out traffic meant there was something of higher priority going on and he needed me to "pay attention".

"2T61- Send rescue to 5640 E Bricks Ave. on a party having a seizure."

"2T61, copy, sending rescue to 5640 E Bricks Ave."

"Break."

I cleared the air (radio air) briefly.

The terminology "BREAK" tells the officers that I am breaking the radio traffic to let officers with priority traffic come on the radio. It also informs them that I have additional information, but cannot stretch it all out in one transmission.

The dispatcher's radio traffic always held priority over the digital transmissions of an officer or firefighter.

Thanks to awesome technology we could see if an officer was attempting transmissions at the same time. If two officers were transmitting at the same time I could raise one officer and have the other break.

"2T61, CPR in progress!"

"2T61, COPY- Rescue is enroute and stepped up to CODE 3."

It was easy to maintain composure. I was actually good at it. Nothing really excited me anymore.

"3T64."

BIG SMILE.

That's my baby. MMM, his voice. So clear. So calm and collected. I would get butterflies in my stomach.

Sometimes I would replay his transmissions and make Jonie listen to his voice. She'd roll her eyes. All in good fun.

I noticed that JT's radio was attempting transmission again, but nothing was coming across the air.

His radio badge flashed on my screen several times.

WALKER

WALKER

WALKER

"3T64- GO AHEAD."

I took a few seconds, and waited for his response.

WALKER

Still nothing from JT.

Silence.

WALKER

His RADIO ID.

WALKER

He has to be pushing it. Or someone is pushing his transmit button.

WALKER

"3T64- GO AHEAD WITH YOUR TRAFFIC."

"3T63- Code 6."

"Break- 3T63- code out on a different channel. I stated quickly and firmly.

I broke the air again, and tried to raise JT on the air.

One more time.

"3T64- I see you are transmitting, but nothing is coming across."

$%^$#&^@&! FUCK. JTW.

Where is your voice? Talk to me.

MY HEART AGAIN. Ugh, an aching stabbing pain in my heart. I felt like I was going to throw up.

I could feel my heart pumping blood. I felt it in my head. My heart beat was so rapid.

My deep fear, it has come true.

WALKER

Everything from the morning was coming true. I lost him. He's gone.

"3T21- TRAFFIC!"

OH FUCK. PLEASE NO. GOD NO.

Maintain your composure SAM. You can do this.

Something is wrong, what the FUCK is wrong.

JTW, don't you dare fucking leave me now. Not now. Not when we are barely starting our life together.

"3T21- OFFICERS DOWN 100th & YORK!"

A scream of horror came across the radio in the Sergeants voice.

"3T21- COPY OFFICERS DOWN. How many ambulances do you want?"

I had to remain calm. For JT, for the Sergeants, for the all the officers that were on. I had to remain calm, because when the world ends, there will always be a 911 Dispatcher.

I was holding in horrific screams from the inside.

"3T21- Start me 3."

3 AMBULANCES?

What the fuck is going on?

I WAS SLOWLY PANICKING INSIDE. I KNEW IT WAS MY NIGHTMARE.

I am ready to escape this and start the day over.

"3T21, Copy, 3 ambulances enroute and I have an airborne chopper on standby."

What's the status of GiGi?

What's the status of my lover?

They are pinned in between cars, I know it. After all, JT escaped death a month before.

Tommy and Brian had been enroute to the area of 100th and York to cover the officer involved accident.

In the moment, I saw my baby stop transmitting.

His button was cleared. He was gone. Silence.

My mind was a mess. I asked a co-worker to send the chopper still, just in case.

I couldn't breath. I unplugged from the radio.

"Sam, Line 9 is GiGi for you."

My coworkers were helpful. It wasn't just impacting me, it was also impacting them.

I answered the phone, I was dreaming.

WAKE ME UP!

Gigi was on the phone for me. She was sobbing hysterically.

"Sam it's JT."

Gigi cried and wasn't understandable.

"Gigi calm down! I thought you were hurt too. Is JT okay? What happened? Gigi is JT okay?"

There was a moment of silence between her and I.

"Gigi? IS JT OKAY?"

"Sam don't tell 20 that I called you. He wanted to be the one to tell you."

Tell me what? Tell me the unthinkable?

Gigi hung up. I still could not catch my breath.

Another coworker yelled across the room to me letting me know that the 20 (SGT) was on the phone for me.

Did I want to pick up the phone? I wasn't ready. After all, I heard the Fire Department air that the Officer was Code Red.

Code Red meant he was in bad medical condition, approaching death if some life saving measures didn't occur. Didn't mean he was dead exactly. Code Black would mean a DOA. Dead On Arrival.

Someone get me the fuck out of here. I want to be on scene. I want to be with JT.

"Sarge? What's up? Why are you calling me?"

Hysteria was tampering with me.

"Is JT okay? Sarge?"

"Sam, JT was in a bad accident."

It was evident that Sarge was in shock.

I went into fight or flight mode.

JT hurt me. He promised me that he wouldn't hurt me.

Is JT alive?

20 told me that Tommy was coming to pick me up. I had no idea what JT's status was.

FEAR.

HE is dead, isn't he?

My world came to a screeching halt. Chaos still ravenous and out of control in the room. 911's blowing up. People reporting the accident. New channels calling in for the report of the accident.

The local news was concerned about the status of the officer. The phones wouldn't stop ringing.

Bar fights, family disturbances, the reports of TOWS/REPO calls, every 911 line blowing up.

I couldn't help anyone, I refused to help anyone ever again. Fuck this shit. I am out.

I closed my eyes. I took a deep breath. I was told once, if you send your thoughts out the Universe would hear it. Much like a prayer.

JT, stay alive baby. I need you. Our babies need you. STAY ALIVE.

Tommy Mr. Tall, Mighty, and Strong, walked in the dispatch center. He was overly distraught. He had been crying. I looked at him with fear all over my face.

"Sam you can't leave until another dispatcher get's here." Stated the newer supervisor on duty.

Tommy gave the supervisor a murderous glare.

"Sam get your shit, we are leaving!"

Tommy meant business. We rushed out of the PD. My high had hit a new low.

WE ran CODE (aka lights, and sirens, emergent, fast as the car will take you) the whole way. I hardly remember the trip. It seemed like forever. Tommy didn't say anything. He was going in to shock. He was way beyond fight or flight He was in the Police Red Zone. He was in a hyper vigilant state.

Tommy was subjected to elevated thoughts also known as hyper alertness. His emotional responses became inseparable from his police role. He wasn't Tommy, my friend, he was Tommy. Tommy was blocking something from me.

Brian stayed at the scene, keeping everyone else safe and wondering if his brother in blue would survive.

Cop work gets in your blood.

—Retired Police Veteran

proposal

"Hey JT!"

GiGi answered her cell phone, ecstatic that her good friend was on the other end.

"Hey GiGi, I hope I am not catching you at a bad time."

JT continued.

"I have been meaning to ask you to do me a huge favor."

Gigi loved JT so much. Not in a romantic kind of way, but in a best friend, brother, work wife, kind of way.

"What's up? Of course, anything, ANYTHING for you."

Gigi knew what I meant to JT. JT had dated a few other people. One included Gigi's childhood best friend. They had lived together for about a year.

JT never seemed enthusiastic about any relationship except for this one.

"She's the one GiGi. I am going to have her ring sent to your house. She has no idea! Don't say anything."

I am kind of a control freak. With that in mind, let's just say it is very difficult to surprise me.

Gigi knew it was coming. It wasn't a shock at all. In fact, she was happy for us. VERY happy for JT.

"I'm keeping it."

"No you are not Gigi. I'll kick your brown ass."

"Fuck you JT- she's way too good for you. You deserve to be happy JT. You deserve happiness."

Her sincerity was truly felt. She had held the secret in for a few weeks.

JT wanted me. I knew it. I could always feel it.

Worth the wait to give you my heart.

— Author Unknown

I must have slipped away into some insane asylum. Insane beings all dressed in white robe like drapes. Blood splatter covered the white walls. It looked as if it had been due to un-controllable cutters or self harmers. Possibly a massacre?

Completely toxic.

BLOOD EVERYWHERE!

I was quickly disillusioned. This was WAY TOO MUCH for one day. This ain't a living. Once again, fuck this shit. I am out.

Stay with me baby. In our reality. Our fantasy.

PLEASE STAY WITH ME.

Tommy walked me in. I was treated like a COP. Like one of the "guys" you could say.

This was what I always wanted. Until this moment. I could never live up to it.

Tommy screamed in rage. A very powerful and commanding scream of rage.

"Where's the asshole that hit my PARTNER!?"

I became tunnel visioned. No account or recollection of the arrival at the hospital. PTSD moment for sure.

Tommy grabbed me by the arm.

"Hey Sam! Come see the high piece of shit that hit Walker?"

I didn't know any better. I was strong, capable, and very fucking angry. After all, if you must commit a crime, drive drunk, drive high, or whatever gets your panties out of a bunch, do so, but DO NOT hurt my family.

I quickly followed Tommy down the hallway. There was a lot of chaos with a lot of hospital staff running. Multiple events, multiple patients.

Tommy's foot steps were still Red Zoned footsteps. We followed a large trail of blood, and a single black tennis shoe lay by the doorway. A creepy hispanic man, wearing a sweatshirt and black sweat pants was on the bed covered by blood. He rocked back and forth in pain. He was screaming. The matching tennis shoe remained on one foot, while the other displayed a bloody, and soiled sock.

This is the piece of shit that hurt my family.

FUCK YOU. KARMA ON YOU.

I forgive you, you must be in a lot of pain? Why did you hit him? Can I forgive him? JT could be dead.

I ignored the passive, and rude comments that came from the pissed off fire fighters.

"Sam!"

I saw a very familiar face. It was re-assuring to know that he was there. Someone I could lean on. Someone I had leaned on over the years.

"I have known you for years, who butchered the tone out on the Officer Down? I sure hope he lives, he's fucked up. Did you know the officer, and why are you here?"

I had known Burke while working with him and his brother at a multiple agency 911 Center.

Burke didn't know JT and I lived together. He didn't know I had even gotten married a first time. Let alone
moved in with JT. We weren't that
close. Just Facebook friends mostly and
we had exchanged emails often regard-
ing work.

There he is!

JT was being pushed in on a gurney
to the open room. I walked away from
the stupid fuck who hit my man, and
from Burke.

JT had blood everywhere!

The hospital was a trauma hospital,
this was a good thing! To the right of
the Emergency Room entrance was an
open room easily accessible for XRAY
and scans.

I ran up to my HEART SONG.

I looked in his eyes. I was horrified, but grateful. This was it. My baby survived. He's a survivor!

He's here to help people. To be God's hands and feet. To do his work for him. Maybe my baby is GOD? Maybe we are all Gods. Sent to love and show love, and BE LOVE.

GiGi ran into the room and was hysterical. She usually was a tough girl behind the badge. TEARS draped her pretty cheeks. They poured from the inner part of her soul. Her best friend/big brother, almost died on her. She grabbed me in despair and desired a hug from me.

I didn't really like hugs, and neither did Gigi. So it was heartfelt.

I just wanted to be held by JT. He just wanted to be held by me.

The Trauma room was quickly bombarded by a staff of doctors and nurses. JT had bright red blood oozing from an open wound on his head. He must have got it from glass shatter. The doctor cleaned him up and stitched his head wound. They started cutting his uniform off.

GiGi and I hurriedly took his duty belt off and his bullet proof vest. It takes forever to break these things in. The last thing JT needed was to have to get fitted for all new equipment.

His duty belt contained his 1911 S&W PD Model. I watched this with close eyes. Gigi gave me the keys to her patrol car so I could secure his belongings in her patrol car.

The chief arrived. The commander arrived. The Lieutenant arrived. Both shift Sergeants arrived.

I finally got to hold JT. He was awake and somewhat vibrant.

You were awake JTW. You lived. My freaking Alien Hybrid.

I HATE YOU! YOU almost died on me.

JT knew I was in shock.

Still surrounded by Brass, Doctor Staff, GiGi, Tommy, The 20's (SGTS). I stood there looking at Joe. He was in so much pain. They took him in to his XRAYS and C-SCANS. Medication started to kick in and solved a little of his pain.

HARSH.

He had bruising appearing all over his body. His knees hurt, his head hurt. His body hurt. His clavicle bone protruded and was shattered. He was screaming on the inside from the pain but remained strong in front of all the Brass.

Finally the meds were kicking in. I could see a little relief in his expression.

The suspect that hit JT, was still screaming in pain. His screams haunted the halls. They echoed and tore apart my heart. They were tearing JT's heart apart.

My eyes locked with JT. I could only breath one slow deep breath at a time. My breath certainly wasn't coming easy.

My hero. Hand in hand until the end. We die together. Deep down I knew, no matter what, in the end, it'd be me and you.

JTW, you melt me.

We have it MADE.

My soul was caressed in this hour of the night. We kissed. He started to speak to me.

HIS VOICE. HIS GORGEOUS VOICE.

The man I fell in love with in bed and over the radio. The man who told me everything. The man who made my heart skip a beat. The man who made my heart beat. MY heart song.

I listened intently and with admiration as JT started to speak to me.

"Samantha August will you marry me?"

I smiled. I caressed his head. No words came out. I was shocked. I choked up from his words. I didn't hear him right. Where was I? I was in shock.

You have put me through a lot of shit you know. I had internal pain that was not discreet. It was evident I was in pain.

I was trying to stay strong for JT. I was trying to stay strong in front of the CHIEF, the SGTS, Gigi, Brian, and Tommy. I wasn't week. Neither was JT.

JT pulled me in closer and tighter.

JT nodded his head and made me look right into his eyes.

"Samantha BABY"

I was locked in again. But quickly shuttered and looked away.

"LOOK AT ME. Don't be scared of me"

I knew he wasn't going anywhere. This was painful. He died on me. My eyes met his again. I was scared. I didn't want to lose him again. I didn't want him to hurt me again the way he hurt me.

"WILL YOU MARRY ME? I am really asking you. I wasn't exactly wanting to ask you to marry me in the middle of an ER, in this condition, BUT I want to live the rest of my life journeying with you. WILL YOU MARRY ME?"

I stood in shock and in pure amazement. Bewildered. Silenced. My hero. A story to be told to our children, and their children. A true love story. Morbid lovers.

My thoughts simmered. I was emotionally exhausted. I was going to get married to my soul mate. I want to feel well and soak this up. This is it. He's asking me.

ANSWER SAM.

Answer.

GET UR SHIT TOGETHER.

Everyone is waiting. Everyone is looking. The Brass made their way to the side of the room to give us our privacy and as a sign of respect.

"JT, baby, don't ever do that to me again. UNTIL DEATH DO US PART."

Until Death Do US Part.

mor·bid (môr′bĭd)

/adj/

1. a. Of, relating to, or caused by disease; pathological or diseased.

b. Psychologically unhealthy or un-wholesome: "He suffered much from a morbid acuteness of the senses" (Edgar Allan Poe).

2. Characterized by preoccupation with unwholesome thoughts or feelings: read the account of the murder with a morbid interest.

3. Gruesome; grisly.

THE END.